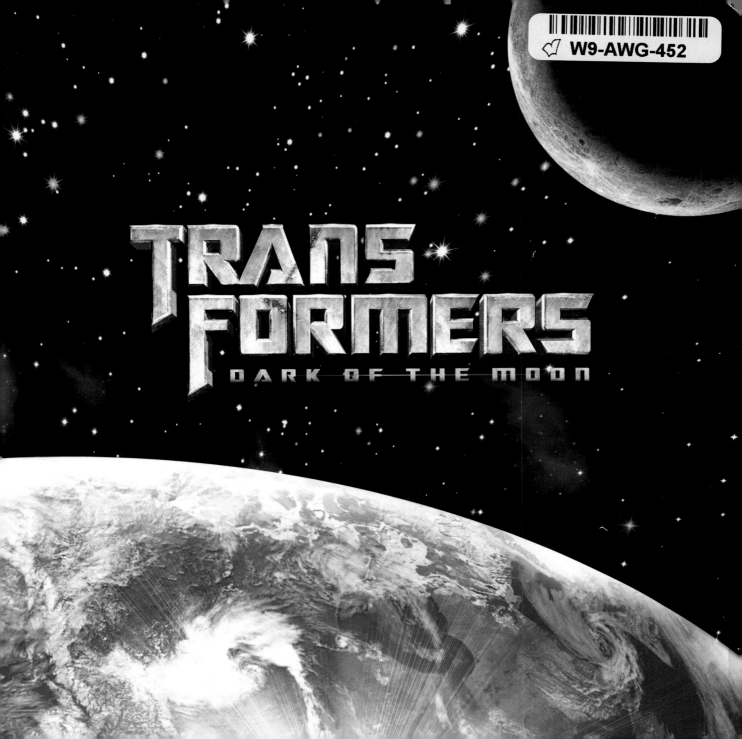

TRANS FORMERS

DARK OF THE MOON

Little, Brown and Company

Hachette Book Group
237 Park Avenue, New York, NY 10017
Visit our website at www.lb-kids.com

Little, Brown and Company is a division of Hachette Book Group, Inc.
The Little, Brown name and logo are trademarks of Hachette Book Group, Inc.

First edition: May 2011

ISBN 978-0-316-18630-8

10 9 8 7 6 5 4 3 2 1

CW

Printed in the U.S.A.

Licensed by:

TRANSFORMERS

DARK OF THE MOON

Autobots versus Decepticons

Adapted by KATHARINE TURNER

Illustrated by MARCELO MATERE

Based on the screenplay by EHREN KRUGER

LITTLE, BROWN AND COMPANY
New York Boston

Transformers have been living on Earth since fleeing Cybertron, their home planet, which had been destroyed by war. The Autobots have a peaceful agreement with the humans, but they know the Decepticons could attack at any time.

Optimus Prime is the leader of the Autobots. He arrived on Earth five years ago with Bumblebee, Ironhide, Sideswipe, and Ratchet. Since then, Wheeljack and Mirage have joined them to defend the people of Earth.

After a Transformers spaceship is discovered on the moon, Optimus thinks the Autobots have found another ally. The Autobot Sentinel Prime is Optimus Prime's old friend and had been stranded on the moon for decades.

Optimus Prime introduces Sentinel to his human friends.

Sam Witwicky has been a friend to the Autobots since they came to Earth, and he spends a lot of time with Bumblebee.

Colonel Lennox leads the NEST team, special soldiers who work with the Autobots to fight the Decepticons.

Sentinel explains to Sam and the NEST team that he had been on a secret mission for the Autobots when his spaceship crashed. He has secret technology—metal pillar devices that can open a Space Bridge.

"The bridge defies the laws of physics to transport matter through time and space," says Sentinel. "We could have used it to ship all the Autobots to a safe haven."

"You could have also shipped soldiers—or weapons," argues Lennox.

Sentinel looks at Optimus. He is not used to small organic life-forms disagreeing with him. "These 'humans'... We call them allies?"

"We have fought as one, Sentinel. I would trust them with my life," says Optimus.

An alarm sounds throughout the base. The Decepticons are coming!
"They want the pillars," says Sentinel Prime. "If they open a Space
Bridge, it will mean the end of your world."

"Get all NEST forces back to base! We're under attack!" Lennox yells into his radio.

Optimus and several Autobots head outside to defend the building.

Ironhide and the NEST team scramble to form a protective ring around Sam and Sentinel. "Keep him guarded!" Sam yells. "He's the key!"

Sentinel looks at Sam. "Yes. As I always have been." Then
Sentinel turns to fire a blast from his cannon at Ironhide.
Sam cries out, "Sentinel, stop! What are you doing?"

"I am a Prime from the great planet Cybertron. I do not take orders from you!" Sentinel says with a sneer. The huge robot grabs the pillars and blasts a hole through the wall. He shifts into a fire truck and zooms out of the building to join the Decepticons.

The Autobots can't believe what has happened.

"Sentinel Prime is a traitor!" Lennox yells into his radio. "Alert the strike teams across the country now! Mobilize the Air Force!"

Sam and Lennox head out with the Autobots to search for the giant alien robot and stop him.

But it's too late. Sentinel Prime has already set up the Space Bridge near the Washington Monument! The pillars float in the sky, forming a ring, and a bright light glows in the middle.

The Autobots arrive on the scene.

Optimus sees his old foe, Megatron, looking battle-scarred from their last encounter. But with Sentinel Prime at his side, Megatron knows he is stronger.

Far above Washington, D.C., on the dark side of the moon, thousands of Decepticons have been hiding for decades. They have been waiting for the Space Bridge to open. They can sense it is time. Five lights glow brighter than all the stars and then form a blinding white circle in the moon's sky. The Decepticons enter the portal, which will take them to Earth.

Behind Sentinel, thousands of Decepticon battle cruisers soar through the Space Bridge.

Watching with glee, Megatron cries, "Here we are! Fight us now!"

Optimus Prime looks at his former friend, Sentinel Prime, and asks, "Why?"

"On Cybertron, we were gods. And here…they call us machines," says Sentinel. "When only one world can survive, you would choose them over us?"

"Just over you," replies Optimus.

Optimus Prime, Bumblebee, Sam, Colonel Lennox, and their friends stand their ground as the Decepticons attack. This will be their biggest battle yet—but they are fighting for freedom and for the future of Earth.

It is their home.